Candyland Moon

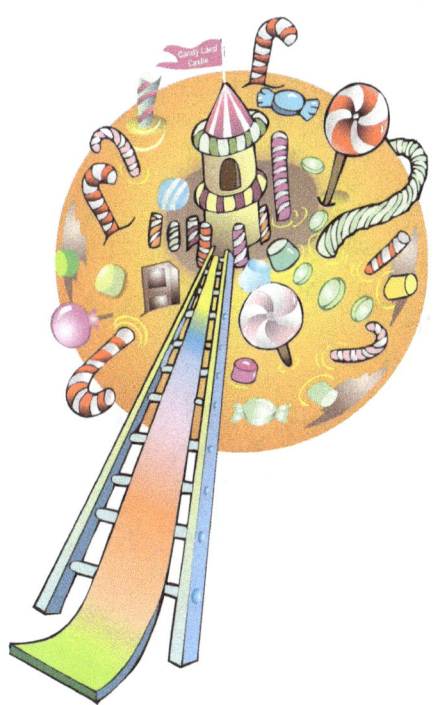

Julie Rose Sparrow

BlueMantle Publishing
www.bluemantle.net
E-mail: info@bluemantle.net

Library of Congress Registration Number: TXU1-907-093

Printed in the United States

Cover art and interor art by Denis Proulx, www.shangrila-studio.com
Cover design and layout by G. Scott Sparrow
Candyland Moon/ by Julie Rose Sparrow

ISBN: 978-0-9665485-5- 6

JUV000000 JUVENILE FICTION / General

JUV029010 JUVENILE FICTION / Nature & the Natural World / Environment

JUV039220 JUVENILE FICTION / Social Issues / Values & Virtues

First Printing November, 2014

Candyland Moon

Julie Rose Sparrow

BlueMantle Publishing
United States of America

For my grandchildren

When Kiran went to sleep one night, not long after her Grandma—whose nickname was Bear—moved far, far away, she was feeling a bit sad and missing her Bear. She lay in bed thinking about all the fun times they had had together and how that would change now.

Other than that, life in Kiran's world was pretty good. Her Mom and Dad were great parents, and she had a nice house with a pool and the best pets a girl could want. She had just started attending a small country school and had made lots of new friends. She was happy. Oh yeah, she had two brothers. They were okay as far as brothers go. Damien, her older brother, thought he was so cool, and he was pretty cool most of the time. He picked on her sometimes.,

though, and she would get so mad at him, but then he would laugh and say he was sorry and play her a tune on his saxophone.

She loved to listen to music and to sing, too! She would sing sometimes while Damien played his sax. Sometimes their mom would sing with them and that was lots of fun!

Kiran's mom had a beautiful voice and sang all the time and played the violin, too. Her little brother Taiowa was a pest, but he was cute and he loved to sing, too, while he played his harmonica. When Bear was still there, she would sing with them, too.

Before Bear left, Kiran would spend the night with Bear a lot, and the two of them would watch movies and eat snacks and drink tea. Sometimes they would draw pictures and color or bake muffins and cookies. It had been so much fun! She loved those times and now she missed Bear so much. She finally fell asleep and had a dream.

Candy Land
Castle

She was sitting on top of a small hill behind her house and leaning up against the trunk of her favorite maple tree.

She was thinking of Bear and missing her. It was night time, totally dark, with thousands of bright stars and two moons.

What, wait a minute she thought, that's not right, two moons?

But there they were—a huge moon that looked like it was so close you could just step onto it and then a small, kind of normal size moon beyond that. The big moon was beautiful and colorful! It looked like a real CandyLand, with candy canes and gumdrops and a castle made of peppermint sticks. This was really weird and awesome all at once!

"Wow," is all she could think to say. Then, just like magic, a ladder-like staircase appeared in front of her and looked as if it went right up to the CandyLand Moon. She looked around and then slowly walked up to it and began her climb to CandyLand Moon.

It took longer than she thought, but she finally reached the top of the staircase. She was standing at the top of a huge rainbow-colored slide that looked as if it was made of ribbon candy. She looked down and stretched out before her were the Wild Strawberry Fields of CandyLand Moon. As Kiran stood on the edge of the platform leading to the ribbon candy slide, she could hardly believe what she was seeing. She was pretty sure she was dreaming, but it seemed so real!

She took a deep breath and sat down on the edge of the platform and on the count of three, whee! She let herself go and down the slide she went, screeching with delight!

Kiran fell off the end of the slide  into the Wild Strawberry Fields and picked herself up and looked around. "Wow!" she thought. She could smell strawberries and chocolate, peppermint and assorted fruits in the bright warm air. The field of wild strawberries was huge, and she saw that there were candy canes like trees and big bushes of gumdrops mixed in with the strawberries. To her left was a huge gumdrop that was black, shiny and sparkling with sugar coating. Past that she saw a river of chocolate, all flowing and bubbly and smelling delicious.

This was really wonderful! She wanted to explore everything. Wondering what she should do next, she happened to glance behind her to see that the ribbon candy slide had disappeared! What?! Oh no, she thought! How can this be? How will I get back home, she wondered?! Well, if it is only a dream then I should be fine, she concluded.

Time to find out and explore this wonderful world!

Just as she started to walk toward the river of chocolate, she saw and heard something strange. It sounded and looked like a small swarm of honey bees headed right for her. She just stood still and waited. As they got closer to her, she noticed that they were a lot bigger than the bees back home and they had cute little faces with smiles on them! "This is weird,"she thought. "I hope they are friendly!"

Just as she was thinking this, the lead Bee spoke and said, "Hello Kiran! We are here to greet you and to help you! We will show you the way to the Peppermint Palace and the Bear Queen. She is expecting you!"

"Ok, pleased to meet you, although I don't know your name," said Kiran.

"Oh! Sorry about that! My name is Honey! Pretty funny, huh?" the bee said, as Kiran giggled and shook her head!

So, off they went walking and flying along the river of chocolate. Kiran chatted with Honey and the rest of the bees and they got to know each other.

"What is the Queen like and how did she know I was coming?" Kiran asked Honey.

"Oh, she is very nice and I'll let her tell you all the rest. See the castle up ahead?! That's Peppermint Palace!" Honey replied.

Kiran did see the castle and it was beautiful! "It looks like it's made of Peppermint sticks, all red and white stripes!" Kiran said.

"That's because it is!" Honey told her.

They came to a drawbridge that went across Chocolate river and right to Peppermint Palace. Kiran was really excited and nervous! As they approached the huge double doors, that looked like chocolate bars, they automatically opened and there stood the Bear Queen, with her arms wide open and a big smile as she hugged Kiran and greeted and thanked Honey and the Bees  for escorting Kiran to the Palace. Honey and the bees left them to go find some gumdrop bushes to pollinate and told Kiran and the Queen they would visit with them later.

"Well, Kiran Rose, what do you think?" asked the Bear Queen. Kiran could hardly believe it! The Queen looked just like her Grandma back home whose nickname was "Bear," except she wore a crown and a pretty purple Queen dress and a fancy cape on CandyLand Moon.

"Wow! I love it! Is it really you Bear?!" Kiran said as she looked at the Queen.

The Queen laughed and said "Yes, Kiran! In my dream life I live here and I am known as the Bear Queen. You, of course, can just call me Bear like you do back home in waking life."

Kiran smiled and hugged her Bear again and then asked, "Am I dreaming too?"

"Yes, Kiran, you are!" the Queen said. "And I have been hoping you would come here and see me in your dreams because I miss you so much! I'm so glad you are here! Come in, I want to show you around and introduce you to some people and animals."

Kiran followed her Bear Queen into the palace. Kiran and Bear went into a private room and sat at a small table and shared a cup of Pumpkin tea, while Bear explained to Kiran what CandyLand Moon was about and how they could always come here when they wanted to. Two huge bears lay sleeping on the floor next to them as a bright orange fire burned in the fireplace.

Bear told Kiran that dreams were the key to CandyLand Moon. "It is a place that anyone can come to when they are really missing someone," she explained. She also told Kiran that to go to CandyLand Moon from now on, all she has to do is to think about going there in her dreams, whether she is dreaming at night, or day dreaming. They are both very important to do and we should all dream as often as we can. "Dreams help us in many ways and sometimes they even come true," Bear said.

She told her that many people come to CandyLand Moon in their dreams and spend time with loved ones that they miss very much. The Bear Queen explained that very little time passes in waking life while a person is visiting

Candyland Moon. Kiran was fascinated and so happy to be there with her Bear.

"Okay Kiran, let's go look around and meet some new friends and grab a bite to eat," said The Bear Queen. Kiran followed her and they walked into a very large room with several long tables filled with all sorts of delicious food! There were people seated all around, eating, drinking, and laughing and talking with one another. There were young kids and older kids and grown-ups too. Kiran and The Bear Queen went to a table at the front of the room and sat down to eat, drink, and talk with the others. Kiran had a wonderful time getting to know people and making new friends!

When they all finished eating and visiting, the Queen stood up and spoke to the room full of people. She

welcomed them all and introduced Kiran to the crowd. Then she told them of a problem that faced CandyLand Moon and asked for their help. The Queen instructed everyone to follow her for a walk around the moon. There was something she needed to show them.

They walked out into the lemon grasses behind the castle which led to the Lime mountains and the Sea of Orange beyond them. There were candy cane trees and gumdrop bushes sprinkled through out the lemon grasses. Honey Bee and her sister Blossom led the way with the rest of the busy bees! Kiran marveled at the Lime mountains with their sugar-capped tops that look just like snow. Three of the mountain tops had what looked like red cherry sauce drizzled on top, and they were the largest of the mountains. Blossom told them they were called the Triple Treat Mountains. As they walked around the base of the Triple Treat Mountains and along the

shores of the Sea of Orange they approached a place that looked like it had once been a jungle, but now was devoid of all color and smelled sour. It looked dead. They all stopped and stared at what was before them and the Bear Queen told them what had happened. She told them that a terrible sickness had come to this part of CandyLand Moon and was spreading through the land. She told them that when the honey bees on Earth started to get sick and die off that it also affected the bees and life on CandyLand Moon.

"We are deeply connected to life on Earth and I need all of you to help me save the honey bees on Earth and CandyLand Moon," said the Bear  Queen. She explained to them that this was what was left of the Jeweled Jungle since the sickness came to CandyLand Moon. The Jungle was a beautiful place of many lush, bright colors and home to the bees, ladybugs, bears and bats that lived on CandyLand Moon. Now there are only two bears left, a small swarm of bees and no one had seen any ladybugs or bats since the Jungle was stricken with the sickness.

The queen said, "We need to bring it back to good health and life!" The two bear sisters that were the Bear Queen's companions, Bonnie and Beth, had been in hibernation mode since the sickness had struck CandyLand Moon. All they did was to eat very little and sleep. They used to take walks with the Queen and run and play in the Wild Strawberry Fields. The bees would bring them honey to eat, but now there was a shortage of honey and bees as well.

Bob Bee, the little brother of Honey and Blossom, said that he thought that maybe some of the bats and ladybugs that survived the sickness were hiding in some underground caves nearby in the Lime Mountains, scared and weak. He was organizing a search party of Bees to look for them and asking the remaining butterflies and fireflies to help them.

The Bear Queen asked everyone to help save the bees and life as we knew it on planet Earth and that would help heal CandyLand Moon, as well. She also reminded them that everything—plant, animal and person—has a place and purpose in life and are very connected.

"Most of the fruits and vegetables that we eat on Earth are dependent on the honeybees to help them pollinate and grow," the Queen said. "Besides making the delicious honey that we all love!"

"How do we do that?" Kiran asked her Bear Queen. Bear told her and all of them to plant lots of flowers when they got home and to spread the word to everyone they knew and to be gentle and kind to the bees and all animals and to try to avoid using poisons.

"If we all do this," she said, "it will help the bees and life on Earth and Candyland moon."

They all thought that was a great idea and would be glad to help spread the word and teach people how to live in peace with bees and all the other creatures. This would make a happy and healthy  life for all who live on Earth and on CandyLand Moon. So they all walked back to the Peppermint Palace and had some pumpkin tea and honey biscuits before they said goodbye to one another. Then all of the dreamers went to their Earthly homes.   Before they left the Bear Queen gave everyone packets of flower seeds to plant and to share with others when they got home.

"These seeds should help get you started on our very important mission! So, be well, do good, and keep dreaming! We will all see one another again soon, if not in waking life, then in our dreams for sure!" said the Bear Queen to everyone.

Kiran walked hand in hand with her Bear Queen as they all walked along the River of Chocolate through the Wild Strawberry Fields, passing the candy cane trees and Gumdrop bushes, to the big Black

Gumdrop and the port key to everyone's home. As Kiran watched the rainbow-colored magic ladder and Ribbon Candy slide appear out of thin air, she was a little sad to leave her Bear and her new friends. But Bear Queen told her she could come back anytime and as much as she wanted, and that made her feel better.

It was almost her turn. The Rainbow slide took everyone to the proper place where they lived, so she hugged and kissed her Bear Queen and said goodbye for now to her new friends. As Kiran was climbing the ladder, the Bear Queen shouted to her to make sure she told Damien, Tai Tai, and Mom and Dad too, about CandyLand Moon, and to come and visit her in their dreams.

Kiran smiled and said she would as she waved goodbye and slide down the rainbow-colored slide back to the hilltop above her home where she woke up in her dream beneath her favorite Maple tree and walked back home with her pocket full of flower seeds and her adventures of CandyLand Moon in her heart.

As she approached home it looked a bit strange. It had a warm glow to it, but she was too tired to take much notice. Kiran floated into her house and to her bed and fell into a deep sleep in her dream before she woke.

She woke up later than usual and felt like she had not slept a wink! Even though she felt she'd been up most of the night, she wasn't tired, she was full of energy and excitement! She ran to the kitchen where the rest of her family was having breakfast and told them about her wonderful dream adventure to CandyLand Moon!

Her Mom and Dad thought it was a wonderful dream and promised to take Kiran to the garden store to get some flower seeds, since she couldn't find the ones she had brought home from CandyLand Moon.

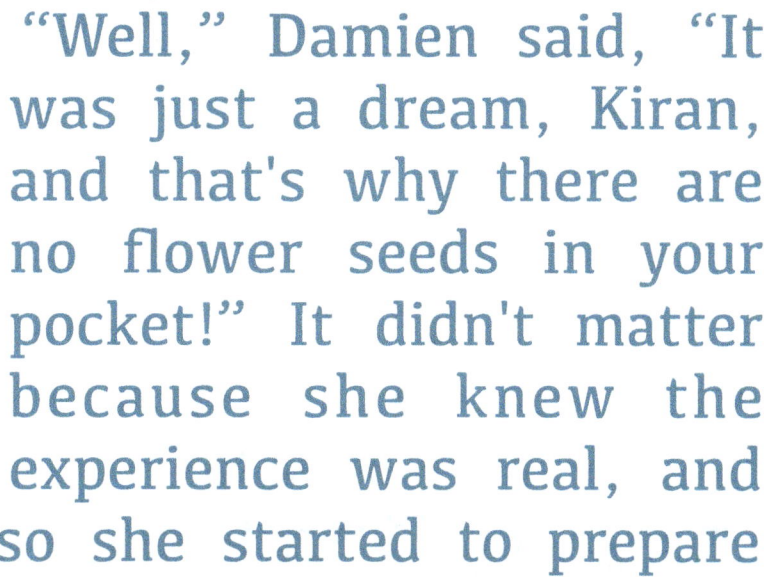

"Well," Damien said, "It was just a dream, Kiran, and that's why there are no flower seeds in your pocket!" It didn't matter because she knew the experience was real, and so she started to prepare the yard for some honey bee flower gardens so she could tell her Bear Queen that she was working on the mission to save the honey bees.

When they went to the garden store Kiran had a list of good plants for honey bees. She picked out seeds for Cosmos, Asters, Lavender, Lantana, and Milkweed. Mom said that would be a good start. They went home and went right to work planting seeds in their gardens around the yard. Damien and Tai Tai helped too. Each of them had their own flower garden and they all bet each other that theirs would be the best one!

After supper and a nice warm bath Kiran was ready for bed, because she was tired from working in the garden. She dearly hoped she would dream of CandyLand Moon again, and be able to go back there soon. She wrote about it in her dream diary that she kept by her bed. She snuggled under the covers and drifted off to sleep very quickly.

Next thing she knew is that she was sitting under her favorite maple tree on the hill by her house and looking up at the huge full moon and thinking of her Grandma Bear and CandyLand Moon. She heard some voices coming up over the hill and then she saw her brothers!

"What are you guys doing here?!" she asked.

"We are going to CandyLand Moon with you!" Damien said. He had his saxophone with him and Tai Tai had his harmonica.

"We figured we could have a CandyLand Band with you as our singer, Kiran!" Damien said.

"Yep, that's right," said Tai Tai.

"Well, ok that's great," said Kiran. "But I don't know if CandyLand Moon will appear tonight."

"Wow, look!, Damien shouted as he  and Tai Tai pointed at the Moon with their mouths wide open! Kiran turned around and there it was! CandyLand Moon! And then she saw the magical ladder that leads to the rainbow-colored Ribbon Candy slide!

They all looked at each other, and Kiran said, "Come on guys, let's go, you

can even go first!" They ran to the ladder and Damien went first, clutching his sax and laughing as he streaked down the slide. Tai Tai went next and held fast to his Harmonica as he, too, went whipping down the slide to CandyLand Moon and the Wild Strawberry Fields, laughing and screeching as he went! Kiran paused for just a moment as she got ready to join her brothers in CandyLand Moon and thought about all the fun and adventures they would have there with Bear Queen and all her new friends.

www.ingramcontent.com/pod-product-compliance
Lightning Source LLC
Chambersburg PA
CBHW081149170626
46809CB00010B/3149